THIN LINE OF CONSCIOUSNESS

SHORT LIFE, BIG STORIES

ASNA

Contents

Thanks to Lord

To my parents, my sister, my brothers and my husband, thank you for your endless encouragement.

I
Thin Line of Consciousness

HAVE YOU EVER wondered how ants live among us? Among Humans? Do they live or just survive? Do they have brains like humans? If they do, what would they feel when they look up to us? Do they look at us in awe? Or would they feel insignificant when they see us selfishly walking around trampling upon their world? Would they hate us when they see our toxic powders destroying their art and soul?

I am Aiza. And I lost my soul when my thin line of consciousness broke.

***

"When people get rejected from all the relevant courses, they take refuge in English Literature.", someone says.

"Nobody demands it these days", some other person says.

"Moreover, you graduated in Economics. Why do want to take English now.", someone else says.

I never thought I had in me the words to write. Now I know.

"You don't need a degree to write, then", comes the reply.

But I set about for it. And then I break like never before.

***

I remember the first day as a Literature student, sitting frozen in my chair, gripping the edges of the writing pad attached to the chair. The criticisms are smiling at my face, scaring me with its fangs and horns. I cover the novel Hungry Tide with my hands and press it hard.

What if I don't get to overcome the tides? They tried to warn me.

I remember Prof. Jignesh's classes. He slaps the novel, Samskara, on the podium soon after entering the class. He flicks his head to toss the strands of his smooth hair that keeps coming to his face. The entire class he makes sure that he tugs his sleeves at the elbows ample times. Then he begins criticising the world. He employs the novel, Samskara, as a means to do the condemnation.

I remember Prof. Hanson. Professor Hanson comes to class with a book and his specs. His neatly tucked-in shirt projects his slight tummy bulge. He adjusts the specs on his nose only when he reads anything from the book. He immediately takes them off with the flair of removing a pair of sunglasses when he looks away from the book to explain things to us. This process happens throughout the period. I notice how his lower jaw clenches and pushes tightly upward when he emphasises accents or tries to stress the English syllables.

I remember the perpetual undertone of a smile on Prof. Hanesh's face when he speaks. A topic opens to let in plentiful other themes. When he sits in the chair before the class and assumes the spirit of a fellow storyteller, I sit with brimming curiosity.

We remember how euphoria takes us high on some days or maybe with some people, yearning for the feeling of contentment to grab us over and over again. But we *distinctly* remember how we are stabbed and ripped off our souls. We *distinctly* remember the sensation if we get to survive after that, always dreading its return in the future.

That's how I *distinctly* remember how my thin line of consciousness broke.

***

"Kindness. Discipline. Humanity. I mean, these are all ingrained into our minds amidst our growth process. A baby born into this world has no idea of these concepts. I mean, it is taught to him. The people raising that baby, and interacting with the baby influence the child. Thus, different compositions of elements of truth form the base for different people differently. This can pave the foundation for their views, opinions and perspectives. That makes different truths. Or beliefs. Right? If that is the case, do these elements hold? I mean... is there any truth in the first place? Everything is taught to you. And me. And different truths for different people. Right? Many of the things you believe and are so dear to you are *taught* to you. I mean, are you even sure your parents are your parents?" Prof. Nijo gives out a terse chuckle.

"I mean, there is no truth. Everything is spoon-fed to you. I mean, by the people around you. By the society. By the media. You have no idea what you are. Why do you want to take over the world? We'll die anyway. You are not achieving anything in life if death is the ultimate truth. Are sure whatever you see is real? You can't trust what you see. Then how can you trust what you don't see?", he runs his hand through his hair. His untied hair fall a few inches above his shoulders.

Then he abandons the podium and starts walking, probably contemplating his words. It seems that way. The repetition of the words, 'I mean', in his speech captures my attention. But what intensely engages me and leaves me momentarily speechless are his words.

I have heard dystopian words before. Read dystopian novels. Read disturbing articles on our existence. Nothing impacted me *negatively*. I am taken aback by the words echoing in my head now. Some random words!

Sometimes words are like a virus. They get into your mind through an invisible path, identify the *perspectives of the life* cell in which your mind functions and then slowly or maybe rapidly gain into the host cell; the host cell of *consciousness*. Once the consciousness cells are tampered with and used to recreate other virus particles in the cell, sometimes even killing the host cell, we get an infection!

"There's no truth? My Ummi taught me to be sympathetic. Kindness matters the most. What you do comes back to you. Do well. Then good will come to you", I find myself mumbling.

Why do I even have to respond to some opinion of a random person?

I pull my lips inward, frowning. My mind takes in the words deeply and starts playing with them. I ruminate the words excessively in just ten minutes and everything starts changing.

Just leave it, Aiza.

There is no truth? No kindness? No sympathy? Made up emotions? Everything is made up?

Everything I believe in? Someone, something created everything up?

It's nothing, Aiza. Just some random words. A play with words to get attention.

And why do I feel like it's getting my attention? Allah!

I look back to see what everyone else is feeling right now, frowning due to a headache. No one seems to be struck by his words. They all seem distracted from the class. Most of them are chatting since Prof. Nijo has gone into a silent zone, filling the class with loud murmurs.

I sit upright and give out a long sigh, causing Prof. Nijo's glance to fall on me. I try to smile with my lips curved inward. That does not affect *his* frowned expression. He glances back at the ceiling.

My parents are mine. What is wrong with him?

I look around the class, perplexed.

I am sitting here, right? That's true. Right?

I give out a nervous laugh. "I am being silly", I murmur.

I am being silly. Right?

Fever. Cough. Core throat. Fatigue. Anything could be a symptom of the virus infection. In my case, my head aches. I cringe from a piercing headache. I am surprised by the rapid propagation of the virus nulling my thought process. I look up at the ceiling and giggle anxiously. I understand the absurdity of the words; some words that whisper the world is overwhelmed with sorrow. But I don't understand the way the absurdity is taking over my soul. Almost instinctively.

You have no idea what you are. What are we all then?

I press my forehead with my index finger and thumb. As the virus feasts inside my head, something starts settling in me. A strange sensation envelops me as a premonition. Something like small pebbles settles in my stomach pit; not just pebbles, but blazing pebbles.

I gulp down, for this form of seething exasperation surprises me. I almost missed Prof. Ashwathy entering the class and would have completely ignored her if Aleena had not tapped on my writing pad to get my attention. It takes everything in me to fake a good morning to her standing up.

I abruptly drop onto the chair when she gestures for us to sit down. I could see Aleena stealing glances at me. But I don't thank her. I ignore her. I find myself questioning everything and everyone.

Is that really Prof. Ashwathy before us? What are you, Aleena? What is everyone doing here? It's all a set-up. Any system is created by someone or the other and everyone else follows. Everything is a lie. What meaning does this all have? We'll die anyway. I have thought about these things before. But why is this bothering me this way now?

Prof. Ashwathy begins a lecture on individualism and then goes on to explain how our identities are created by other people. But my focus is on the black and white patches on Professor Ashwathy's flowy saree.

"Life is black and white. You fill it with fake colours of hope, love and religion which are all made up just to make life easier to live", Prof. Nijo commented a few days back. I shook my head in disapproval that day. Now I am shaking my head, for the colours start fading within me.

Black and white world. No love, huh?

I wonder whether Prof. Ashwathy knows that I am disregarding her class on 'individualism', and for the first time in my life, I seem not to care about the possible disgruntlement I might cause to someone. This surprises me even harder and I feel like the hot pebbles are accumulating faster inside me now.

No Aiza. There is love. Kindness. You are here and that's true. Don't listen to trivial utterances. The world has its colours.

"Do you star gaze?" Prof. Ashwathy asks and then pulls her lips inward. Everyone gives a positive reply to it. I ignore her question, my mouth agape from the growing heaviness within me.

"What do you feel?", she asks, her eyes linger on my face for a while. I don't react. Slightly bending forward, I glance down at the dusty hemline of my long black purdah, hugging my stomach tightly. She turns back to the class.

"Peace.", Aleena responds.

"Beauty", answers Bhanu.

"Peace and beauty", says Ann.

Prof. Ashwathy stands behind the podium, analysing the answers with a firm look on her face.

"Insignificance", comes Alan's reply.

"Yes!", she says in delight. "Insignificance! Exactly! Everything below seems null and insignificant. We are nothing up there. Like ants down here."

Like ants down here.

You know, the replication rate of the virus and the ability to evade the immune system can decide the strength of its spread. This virus seems to know how to well play, I suppose. The immunity of my thought processes staggers as the virus stunningly replicates and plays inside my head with words.

SOME. RANDOM. WORDS.

The effect of the infection percolates down to my heart. Everything seems new and vague to me now. I question why I should get this education. I question why I believe the things I believe. I doubt the significance of life. *My life.* Everything is happening so fleetingly. The poison is diffusing within my head so fast that I struggle to compose my thoughts.

Like ants down here.

When the bell rings, I shove my books into my bag with trembling hands, neglecting my pens and a pencil before me. I swiftly get up, sling my bag over my shoulders, and sprint out of the classroom. I walk briskly on the veranda to quickly get past the window of my classroom, outpace Prof. Ashwathy on the way and stride out of the college. I look up at the bright sky when I am out of the College gate, and I shudder at the first thought that surfaces instantly in my head.

Is this sky real?

***

After Magrib namaz I resume to sit on my legs. I have been in this position for almost an hour. Soon Ishah adhan will be heard. I roll a white bead of the rosary with my index finger and thumb. I could see Ummi setting the table for dinner through the tiny opening of the door. Uppa is already at the table with his plate. I keep the rosary down and look at the namaz mat.

I take a deep breath and try to get up; try to haul the heavy heart up. I struggle as I push myself off the namaz mat. My legs tingle from sitting too long and my heart has successfully built up a tremendous rock with blazing pebbles. I find it hard to stand, so I plop onto the bed behind me. As my mind continues its roller coaster ride, I find the pain growing more and more intense inside me. I hear Ummi's voice from outside the room.

How do I tell them that their daughter is doubting whether they are her parents?

I roll onto my back not caring to change my white namaz attire.

I don't know whether that Ummi is my Ummi. Uppa is my Uppa. They taught it to me. If everything is a lie and everything ends, why should we even bother to live? Why do we chase after this life? Why do I have dreams?

If nothing matters, then I don't matter. If I don't matter, why do I live? Why do I live?

I can even end my insignificant life. My Insignificant Life!

Like ants down here.

I abruptly sit up, panting, for the dangerous turn of my thoughts scares me. Suddenly I find myself distrusting me. I don't trust me anymore. My whole body shakes as terror engulfs me and then starts strangling me. I find it hard to breathe and the first drops of tears exit my eyes. Then unknowingly I start bawling. I ask myself whether to call out for Ummi like I always do when I am just sad, but this time I am questioning if she is my mother. And that makes me sob even harder.

The sound of my relentless sobs brings Ummi and Uppa to the room. I try to explain but all I can manage is some babbling. I can see the concern in their confused eyes. But beyond a shadow of a doubt, I can say I am more confused than them.

How do I make them understand this feeling?

Ummi pulls me to her, holding me firmly. Even as the tears continue to form and rush down, the rock in my heart does not move an inch. A numbness spreads through my skull and I pass out.

*****

Ummi once told me that sleeping is like a small death; you are in the world but not *consciously in the world* when you're sleeping. She keeps reminding the family that sleep keeps you away from living. So, to live more, sleep less. I used to remind myself to live more and sleep less. But now I yearn for sleep. And sleep only. I sleep to evade from life.

I can see the change of mood in my house because of me. I cling to my bed these days. I am the only subject they recurrently discuss now. I am the only concern they have now. My siblings try to engage me in conversations and I respond with muteness. But I can't care and I don't care. When I wake up from sleep, all I yearn for is the next sleeping hour. I once gathered the guts to get back to my dream chair at college and I ended up embarrassing myself. But I don't seem to care about it either.

When nothing makes sense, we stop valuing things. When we stop valuing things, we stop caring about anyone or anything. And that frightened me.

I *distinctly remember* the day I went back to college. But soon I was taken to the staff room, for I found it hard to breathe inside the classroom.

"What is it, Aiza?" Fr. Thomas, head of the dept., asked me, surprised and a little shaken. I know he had big expectations. I replied in tears and no words.

"Talk, Aiza. What is happening?" Prof. Hanson took his turn in inquiring about my situation. I felt like a criminal under interrogation.

"Nothing makes sense. This institution. Education. Why do we all live if we are to die later? No kindness. No humanity. Nothing. Everything is taught to me right?", My weeping made the words slurry but he got the words. *He got the words only.* He did not understand the terror underlying those words.

His face wrinkled, probably because of confusion.

"Aiza, this is a sea you got yourself into. Maybe the course scared you. This is nothing you've learned so far. So the tides are drowning you. You need to learn to swim against the tides."

Oh. No. Allah. Not the course. I admired the course. It's not...

"Read a lot. New books. Learn new concepts every day."

Why? Why should I read books? New concepts? If it is taught to me, then it is made up by someone. Will that become truth? OH. ALLAH. HOW DO I MAKE MYSELF CLEAR? How is everyone calm here? Do they not know these are all nothing?

"That's how you learn. Crying and roaming on the veranda here will not calm you down. Take this opportunity to enlighten you.", Prof. Hanson made a face and tone when he mentioned the part I cried too much. I tried to calm myself down by pursing my lips, to contain sobbing. His annoyance with the way I was behaving hit me. I went home after that. And decided not to come back ever.

***

The headache is constant now. The rock in my heart is still well-built. The infection inside my skull is persisting. I am still a wrecked soul.

It's been a month now since I have gone to college. Uppa has already informed the college that I quit. I wonder how Fr. Thomas feels about it. But I don't care and I hate myself for not caring. The sound inside my skull gets so deafening and fierce that I force a pillow against my head too hard to silence it every night, weeping.

I sleep beside my Ummi now and I don't feel sorry for my Uppa, who sleeps on the couch now. I hate myself for that too.

"I would do something stupid if I slept alone", I told Ummi a few days back, weeping. She wept with me that day.

I roll up my top's sleeves and keep it in place above the elbow to perform ablution. I still do namaz, for it is the only thing in my life that connects my frozen body with my broken soul. The rest of the time I feel detached from everything and everyone. I feel detached *from my soul.*

I glance up at the sky through the square grills of the window in the patio area behind the kitchen. Between the two tall buildings behind our home, a small rectangular portion of the sky is visible. I roam my eyes on the small part of the sky that can be seen. It's time for the Asar namaz. The soft murmurings of prayer from the masjid nearby fill the air.

Winking a few times, I look down and just when I am about to open the tap, I see ants marching in a procession on the adjacent wall.

They live in elegance not caring about their insignificance. Why can't I do that? Like ants down here.

After taking ablution, I rush to get to my prayer mat. I wish that it was the Ishah prayer, the night prayer, so that I can get back to bed early; not that I sleep well now but the idea of sleeping attracts me.

When Ummi comes looking for me, I am reclining on the mat after namaz, clad in the white namaz purdah. My body does not move an inch, except for my eyes. Ummi lowers herself and sits beside me; positioning her back against the cot behind us. She places a book and a pen near me. My forehead lightly creases but I remain silent.

"Do you want to talk?" she asks, concerned.

Nothing will exist. Then why talk?

A numbness has taken over me excessively and I don't particularly feel anything these days, except for the heavy rock in my heart.

"Write what you feel if you can't talk about it. Can you do it?", she searches for any sign of approval. None she gets. I lay like a frozen corpse. Her nose reddens as her eyes moisten.

"Can *I talk, then?*" She pleads.

Save it. We'll die anyway.

She wipes her nose and the flowing tears away with the back of her hand. When her tears don't strike me like they used to strike me before, I shudder.

She does not wait for me to give the consent.

"I had a classmate when I was doing my pre-degree. Sajda", she begins, smiling with the tears. "I used to look up to her a lot. She was beautiful. Rich. Great family. Good in studies. Everyone loved her. I wanted to be her in a lot of ways. In every way. You know, Aiza, I remember peeking at her whenever she was around. But after a year I met her, she was diagnosed with cancer... Things started to change after that."

Staring with wide eyes at the rosary on the floor, she reminisces, while my gaze stays unfazed on the book lying beside me.

"Everything changed about her after that", she says. "Imagine I'm a wall made of bricks."

She brings her hand onto the prayer mat on which I am lying and draws small rectangular boxes with the tip of her index finger. "A wall..." she whispers. She closes her eyes as though to contain the rush of emotions in her.

"The first time I saw her after her diagnosis, the topmost layer of my wall broke. Her sunken eyes and slimming figure whacked me right at my face. It's funny a person who barely noticed me and barely talked to me could shatter my wall just like that", she sniffs and then resumes,

"My wall started to fall off layer by layer as she slowly started dwindling. And the debris started to accumulate in my heart every day. It might be because she inspired me a lot. Or maybe I imagined myself in her position quite a lot of times. Or maybe I dreaded that what happened to her could happen to me and my loved ones. I don't know why and how a situation or a person could shatter my wall and load those broken pieces into my heart in such a devastating manner. But it happened. I went down with her and I doubt whether she even knew my name", she gives a terse shivering laugh.

"I had noticed Sajda's absence in all exams. It was my Uppa, your grandfather, who came home from his work one day, a few days after our exams, and informed me about her death... and then..." she stops. She remains silent for a minute. My eyes slowly raise to hers. I see her chin shivering, and her eyes seem far away somewhere.

"It became black everywhere. Black! I still don't know how I managed to get back to my room before I broke down. Everything felt new and so little. So meaningless. Felt the world so meaningless. *I* felt meaningless in this world. Thought I was going to fade away so fast. A terror slithered through my whole body and all of a sudden the world seemed so cruel and painful", she shakes her head as though she still finds the feeling too overwhelming.

"I lost my consciousness. I was taken to the hospital, for I cried all day, grew delirious at night, and stopped talking to people. It was like suddenly I started smelling death on everyone. On me. I was a wrecked site as the last layer of my wall tumbled down and I felt so exposed to the scorching world that I suffered from burns across various parts. I yearned for a tablet that would give me my consciousness back. *My life back...* After the intense painful days, I grew numb", She pants as if there isn't enough air in the room. Her eyes abandon the rosary and fall on my face.

I grew numb.

"I felt invisible", she says as tears start to take their course down her cheeks again.

I abruptly turn my face to her and then raise myself to sit beside her, gasping for air. My frown deepens as I start to sob along with my Ummi.

"I know, Aiza. Sometimes we don't need to survive a tsunami or witness an earthquake to feel traumatized. Sometimes we lose our minds for nothing. Sometimes little careless things, random people and random words can hurt us. Drown us. I know how you feel. Aiza, you are adamant now that the world is heedless to your words. To your feelings. But trust me. I KNOW.", she resumes panting, her moist cheeks and runny nose glimmering.

How? Please, ALLAH, how?

"Aiza. What are you afraid of?" Ummi examines my face, sniffing.

Ants. Or being an ant in this universe.

"I was afraid of oblivion. Becoming invisible. To face death. You know..." Just then the Maghrib adhan echoes through the air. Halting her words midway, she shuts her eyes firmly. I start to weep vigorously and my Ummi opens her eyes quickly, feeling disquiet.

After the adhan, she murmurs a prayer. My prolonged weeping makes my head and heart ache even more.

"It took me two months to come back to life. Too long months. In these two months, I died every day. First, the pain killed me and then later numbness killed me. But Aiza, when I came alive after that, I was different. In a better way. It was a slow process. But I got through it", Ummi reveals. She seems calm now.

"Yes, I felt invisible. But I was becoming invisible to myself. I was not invisible to the world. And by 'world', I don't mean the universe you are thinking. My world is my Ummi, my Uppa, my sisters, and everyone I care about. You might not even be a speck in this universe but you can be a universe to your people. And that matters. A lot. And trust me, Aiza, you are a universe to me. To your uppa. To your brothers. Azia, your sister imitates you because she wants to be you", Ummi gently pats on my head a couple of times. I cry even more intensely.

You might not even be a speck in this universe but you can be a universe to your people.

"You don't have to be seen and understood by the world. It's impossible. But become a universe to your people. Let kindness thrive everywhere you go. That's how you learn to live. There is kindness, Aiza. There is love. Love is the universe. And if someone comes and says that it is all made up, it won't stop being there... Love, kindness, and humanity will always be there. It's just a matter of realizing or not realizing it."

Love, kindness and humanity will always be there. It's just a matter of realizing or not realizing it.

"Next time when someone comes and tells you that there isn't any truth, feel pity for that person. But don't believe it. You know it, Aiza. YOU. KNOW. IT", Ummi looks into my puffy eyes and then swallows with difficulty.

So, it's OK being an ant?

My sobs have receded now to sniffing. I glance down at the notebook on the prayer mat. I quickly grab the notebook before I change my mind and start scribbling. First, my words come composed, but as I proceed, I feel the rock inside me shaking. And my body shakes too from its heaviness. I start sobbing again. My head gives way to a roar and the deafening sound heats my ears, causing me to crinkle my face.

I find myself no longer writing, rather I am scratching and gouging the paper with the tip of the pen. I let out a howl as I fall onto my Ummi's lap, frantically. I lay there, weeping for minutes. I fall asleep from the exhaustion. And for the first time after that terrifying day, I get a pleasant dream in my sleep.

You might not even be a speck in this universe but you can be a universe to your people.

***

I lay on my back under the mango tree in the front yard of our maternal home. I can hear my siblings and cousins playing Blind Man in the living room. The light finds its way through the lush foliage of the tree and falls on my face. My head is slightly turned right to gaze at the clear sky adorning the background of the tree. Birds make beautiful flights across the vast sky.

How is this beauty even possible?

There was an Aiza who broke, and feared the tremendousness of the sky and died. There is an Aiza who has been moulded, honours the greatness of the sky and is awakened. My line of consciousness has been revived. And it is not thin anymore. My revived immunity cells of consciousness keep in mind the kind of virus that invaded my head and squashed my old consciousness. The word 'depression' scares me even now. But that's OK. I need it to remind myself about a lot of things.

I can now look up to the sky and realize the colours. I don't have to be recognized by the universe. I have to become a universe for others. I pity those who spread the idea of a vague, black-and-white world. I wish they could see what I see. I see the colours. And during the times when the colours fade around me. I will become colourful for others.

II
None Of My Business

I AM LATER than usual today. The lane leading to our gate easily enters dark mode when dusk sets in, thanks to the high-rise buildings and tight-knit houses. The light on our tiny porch is on. I know it is still flashing because of me. I sit on the verandah and slide my foot out of my shoes. Before I stir to get up, I catch sight of the waste bin outside the gate. I did not notice it at the gate when I came in today. To be precise, I don't notice it any day. Because taking it outside when it is full or inside after it gets emptied by the corporation people, is none of my business.

It's my Mom's business. The rim of the waste bucket is filthy and has developed black patches. I think of the moments I caught my Mom scraping off the black filth formed inside and around the waste bucket. I remember the air reeking of rubbish. Then I think of my Mom touching the bucket. Her fingers curled on the filthy rim of the waste bucket; breathing the stinky air. I scrunch up my nose and scratch the back of my head.

The door is still not locked. It is because of me. These days when I am late, I get inside to the noise of dishes being washed. Or I see Mom wiping the table. Or I see my Mom mumbling prayers sitting on the prayer mat. Or I hear my parents chatting. The last two are pleasing to enter into, for I see my Mom relaxed. Of course, she seems calm while doing *her* job. But it pesters me when she does the job alone. I never joined her. But it disturbs me.

Today I see my Mom on her prayer mat clad in a loose white namaz dress that covers her whole body save for her face and palms. She is gazing down at the mat, preoccupied. And suddenly I do what I do since I was a kid. Sliding my leather sling bag onto the floor, I shrink onto her lap. God! The feeling! As she begins caressing my hair, I feel the scorching tensions in my head retreating; the tensions stimulated by today's work, situations, people, and the thoughts of my unfulfilled dreams. But I am grateful for the cure beneath my head. Nothing else works. At least not the way this one works. I close my eyes to embrace this warmth and unknowingly I doze off.

It's 6 a.m. as I scroll on my phone. Last night I dreamt of the green waste bucket. I cannot say it was green exactly. I was painting the bucket using a black crayon in the dream. The bucket was fully tainted in black in the end. My mind just would not stop roaming around this stupid dream. By that, I don't mean the rubbish bucket. But this fact: I don't even try to change by doing things that should be done by me. At home. *But it's none of my business. Right?*

Lazy may not be a strong word. Maybe it's disgust. Again, is that an overstatement? Either way, I find it hard to clear up or even help clear the mess everyone here together creates. The mess even I am a part of. Our filthy waste bucket holds the rubbish I throw in too.

I scrub my eyes with my fingers as I feel uneasiness creeping into me.

It's partly because I feel disquiet when I see my Mother doing it for everyone. Everyday.

Everyone acts like it's none of their business.

And it is also partly because I get irritated when I cannot bring myself to help her. The funny part is: that I can cook once. Or do dishes. Or do laundry. Or mop the floor. Or at least wipe the kitchen countertop. Or just set the table. Too many options. Why am I still feeling the urge to start the change by taking that nasty bucket in and out of the home? I suppose I want to. Just once. To touch that filthy rim as my mom does. It takes courage, I suppose.

"He who is not conquering some fear has not learned the secret of life", said Ralph Waldo Emerson. My biggest fear right now is my hands coming in contact with the waste bucket at home. People probably would laugh at that. But I am wrinkling my face at the very thought.

I roll onto my side before I pull myself away from the bed. My eyes scan if there is anyone around when I descend the stairs. Unlike the bucket that is settled on the far end beside our gate, my mind feels unsettled. But thanks to the lid that is in place, I don't need to see its interior. The green color has faded over time. I think of the dream where I color the bucket black. A moment passes as I stand there regarding the black patches formed on the rim and the bottom of the bucket. I let go of a long and heavy sigh. Then I sigh again. Then I keep sighing.

After doing enough sighing exercises, I find myself holding my breath as I begin to lower myself to reach the rim. The moment my fingers touch and curl into the inner curve of the rim, I instantly regret it. My fingers feel sloppy. Partly because my palm is now sweating. And partly because of the greasy surface my fingers are now in contact with. My face begins to get a red tint as my lips grow pale from the pressure I instill not to breathe. I am no longer walking. I run to rid of the bucket in my hand.

I almost knock over the bucket when I throw it onto the floor. My Mother looks up from the coconut grater. Her eyebrows move apart as her eyes run from me to the slithery waste bucket and then again back to me.

"Seriously, Mom! How do you do it?" I whine as I vigorously wash my hands in the kitchen sink with the dish soap.

She resumes grating the coconut but her gaze is still on me. I don't see the smile that has now lit her face as I continue to wash my palms with the iron scrub.

"Do it. Tomorrow. And after that. And after that. And after that." She speaks over the grating noise. "You will understand how I do it, Ashiq."

I don't respond to that. I scoot upstairs, frustrated.

I take the bucket in the next day. I still don't comprehend her capability of doing that. Or after that day. Or after that day. Or after that. Or after that. Or after that. My stomach continued to churn after touching it. Eating is hard now without thinking about the rim. Pale green slippery rim! But I resume doing it. Again. And again. And again. And a painful month passes!

***

It's easier now. And I never walk past the bucket ignoring it now. I understand how my Mother does it. Although I took more duration to realize it than the time she suggested. *Habit.*

Habits flow with us. Or maybe it's more like we flow with the habits we ingrain in us.

It would be a lie if I said that I don't sit smugly when my Mom asks my siblings to learn from me. But it's more about the other joy I experienced. Still experiencing after I conquered something I have loathed ever since I remember. Our gross rubbish tin! Now that I have moved past it, I identified my next fear to conquer. I am looking at my new fear. The yellow-tinged toilet bowl.

Gosh, Ewww!!! How does my Mom do it?

III
Fountain Pen

AMAR PINS KHALID against the wall with a thud.

"What have you done to make Ummi and Uppa love you this much?" Amar utters with gritted teeth.

Khalid, though terrified, does not struggle to get free; his legs barely touching the ground. He cringes in pain as his brother squeezes him against the wall, causing him to tap consistently on the hand gripping him. Amar smirks at the thought of how effortlessly he could squash his twelve-year-old brother. He then throws him at the wooden stool right in front of the locked door. Khalid's forehead bumps against the edge of the stool. The impact ejects a suppressed shriek from him. A sharp pain shoots through his head causing him to squeeze his eyes shut.

Amar is surprised by the contentment filling his heart.

How long he has been waiting for this moment! Alone with his brother. How many times has he wished that his parents stood by his side! *For once.* How many times he wished he had his brother all by himself! *For once.* His Mother meddles in all matters concerning Khalid. *Always.* And she never leaves them together. *Never.* But today she had no choice.

Their father had to attend a meeting at the Juma Masjid, Kozhikode. Concerned about his return alone at night on the train, she accompanied him. But she was mainly concerned about her kids at home if she left. But she did anyway.

"Amar, please don't fight with your brother" His Mother knew. That's why she kept saying that before she left.

Amar slowly nodded, pretending to be asleep.

She then left to peep into the room where Khalid slept peacefully, opposite Amar's room. *His parents' room.* Khalid sleeps in their room even now.

"You will kill him in his sleep!" she shouted when Amar argued about that once. "I don't understand why you show no mercy towards your brother"

Amar cannot particularly pinpoint anything that would explain why he hates his brother. He hates him. That's it! No particular reason. But deep down he knew it all started when he saw the nurse passing the newborn baby boy into his Mother's hands when he was just five. *To his Mother's hands.*

"I don't know, Bhaiyya. Why do you hate me like this?" Khalid mumbles despite the numbness in his head. He still finds it hard to keep his eyes open.

Amar scoffs in response. Nevertheless, the blood dripping onto his brother's T-shirt concerns him.

Should I get rid of that T-shirt before Ummi comes? But the wound on his forehead will reveal everything anyway. One more cause for her to dislike me and one more reason to love him a lot more!

It brews inside him to give another blow to his brother but the cut is already pouring out too much blood, so he manages to stand with closed fists.

"Where did you get the money?", Amar asks firmly. "You stole it, huh?"

Khalid's eyes widen when he sees the coin box Amar has hoisted in the air. He gulps down before answering,

"Bhaiyya, ummi gave…", Khalid begins to clarify.

"SHUT…UP…", Amar's sharp voice reverberates through their tiny house, causing Khalid to swiftly rise and retreat from his brother. Khalid stares in disbelief at his brother who is seething with anger.

"Ummi gave.. Ummi said…Ummi…Ummi…Ummi! Just shut up, ok!", Amar pants heavily; clenching his teeth while clasping the coin box in his hand.

Words get stuck in Khalid's throat, terrified about the possible retort if those got out. As his chin begins to tremble and tears start to fill his eyes, Khalid buries his face in his hands. Even as he weeps, he makes sure he sniffs without making much noise, worried the sound might trigger more anger from his brother.

The door slamming sound startles Khalid and he abruptly uncovers his face. Finding that his brother has vanished into his room, he resumes sobbing. Too many words and countless thoughts slip through his head as tears immoderately dampen his cheeks. He leans against the wall, shattered. The pain in his heart mostly comes from the defeated feeling that has now settled in his stomach pit.

An hour passes.

An hour passes as he stands rooted to the spot. An hour passes when he realizes that his legs won't hold him anymore. But it only takes an hour for him to decide on the next big step of his life. *His defeated twelve-year-old life.*

Amar blinks a dozen times to come to terms with his surroundings. He checks the small timepiece on the round plastic table top near his bed. Its ten minutes past noon time. He scrunches his face as he realizes he has been slumbering for hours. As he stretches himself on the bed, he suddenly catches himself thinking of the cut on his brother's forehead.

Did I go too hard on him? Somebody should go hard on him. Right?

He sits up and stretches his arms again. Just then he realizes the fan is not on; that explains why his entire body is soaked. But he wonders what can explain the total hush in the home. Perched on the top of a moderately steep hill, their minuscule home is away from the hustle down the road. Their only neighbor is an old lady who spends most of her time sitting on her front porch like a mute ascetic. But this total absence of any sound seems new and annoying to Amar.

His stomach makes a rumbling sound reminding him that he has not eaten anything today. He prepares to go to the kitchen, for his Mother has already cooked lunch in advance before she left. Just when he slides out of the cot, he sees a thin notebook on the pillow next to the one he had been using.

A piece of paper is cello taped on its cover. Amar slants his head to read the words on the paper, written with a considerable gap in between each letter. 'M y B e s t F r i e n d'.

He curiously reaches for it. Taking the book in his hand, he turns the cover page to find the words, 'This is Amar bhaiyya, Khalid's diary.

Wiping the sweat beads on his forehead, he sits back on his cot and turns the page.

MARCH 3, 1997

Today is my birthday. Uppa gifted me this notebook today morning. He liked my idea of making this my new diary. He said that I could even name my diary. I did not have to think for long. I knew. I am calling it Amar Bhayya. And I will tell it everything I want to say to my Bhayya. I lied to my Bhayya even today. Uppa gave me a pen too with the notebook. I placed it on Bhayya's table and told him that Uppa asked me to give it to him. I lied. I gave him that because I wanted to give him something to make him happy. And immediately I ran after that, for I was scared he would throw it at me like he does most times when I give him anything. I was happy today because I saw him writing with that pen later.

March 7, 1997

Today I heard Amar Bhayya asking Ummi for a fountain pen. Ummi said it would cost too much. She asked him to write with the pens at home. What can I do? I will ask Uppa for some money for it. But how much money should

I ask?

March 9, 1997

I have 2 rupees now. Ummi said that I could keep the change left after I bought the milk packets yesterday. I wanted to buy Imili candy with the money but what if Amar Bhayya still wants the fountain pen? I should get it for him. I will buy Imily candy later.

Amar squints as drops of sweat slip from his temples and drips into his eyes. Wiping his face with the back of his hand, he gazes nervously at the notebook. Amar flicks quickly through the pages where his brother had recorded the subtle climb in his savings for the fountain pen. He realizes why Khalid always eagerly probed whether the milk got over in the house. Amar always suspected it to be his brother's tactic to get outside to play with his friends down the hill. It surprises him as his heart starts aching for no particular reason.

Why am I feeling this distraught? Is this what guilt feels like? No. He is a pervert. He stole all the love my parents once gave me.

He turns the pages and abruptly stops at the page showing yesterday's diary entry.

June 11, 1997

I am really happy today. I have 30 rupees with me now. Mammalikka showed a fountain pen in his shop when I went to his shop to buy milk two days back. He said he would give it to me if I could manage at least 30 rupees. I have not told anybody of my plan. Tomorrow Ummi and Uppa will not be here. I am afraid to gift him when they are here. I am afraid they would say 'see what your younger brother did for you', 'you always hate him but look at him'. I just hope they would stop talking about me in front of him. But tomorrow is big. Amar Bhayya will stop hating me. He would smile at me. I know. He will do it. We will become friends after that. TOMORROW WE WILL BE FRIENDS.

Amar suddenly realizes he has been holding his breath all this time. And when he breathes, he feels like he is not getting enough air into him.

'Tomorrow we will be friends'

The coins were his savings for me. Everything he did and wrote in his diary revolves around me.

Amar purses his trembling lips as he seeks all the possible ways he could justify his actions. He feels dejected as he finds none.

One more entry is left in the diary. He shudders for no *particular reason*. It was written a few hours ago.

June 12, 1997

10:00 AM

Maybe I can't make you happy, Bhayya. Maybe I am the problem. If I am gone, will you be happy?

"No...", Amar whispers with trembling lips.

Maybe I should go from here. Then Uppa and Ummi will see you. Like really see you. Like the way you want.

"No..." he widens his eyes as his vision blurs; not from the sweat this time but tears.

I am running away. I don't know where to. But I am scared. But I am running away. Will you love me if I run away? Bhayya?

"No... Khalid." Tears start to escape his eyes. As assorted emotions and diverse thoughts drown him, he finds his heart sinking. He can't remember the last time he called his brother by his name and the name, 'Khalid', seems foreign in his lips now.

Why Khalid? I am sorry. I am sorry. Sorry. Sorry. Sorry.

Though his trembling lips cannot form comprehensible words, his heart keeps apologizing; for no *particular reason*.

When ummi and uppa return...

Without delay he throws the notebook on his table, overturning the jug on it. The water spills onto the pages of the book, soaking up the words in it. Amar darts out of the room and out onto their front porch. He stops himself when he sees the old woman planted herself on the steps opposite their home. The old woman pulls her stained pale white Chiffon saree pallu and tucks it between her knees to prevent it from falling off her head.

When she glimpses him, she lifts her index finger to point down the hill; frowning. With a frantically beating heart, he darts down the hill; tripping a couple of times. His chest aches and he feels like it would explode. But he keeps running. His legs get heavy and drained. But he keeps running.

When the sun decides to settle down, its crimson shades cover the sky. Birds twitter hysterically as though to ward off the silence engulfing the tiny houses on the hill. The main door of the empty house sways with a squeaking sound as the occasional wind blows against it. The old woman remains motionless peering at the path two souls have disappeared hours ago.

IV
Anwar

ASHRAF PUTS ON the cotton blue shirt for the third time unwashed, ignoring the laundered shirt Arifa, his wife, has placed on the chair arm in their room. He anxiously sets out.

"Drive slow. Be careful", his wife cries. But he is too gay to take the words into him. After half an hour, he halts his car in front of an aged, roofed house. He is striding to the tiny house, infested with mold, when he spots Kabeer giving him a fixed gaze. Ashraf gives out a long breath with a pout, anticipating the words behind that look.

The moment he faces Kabeer, he hastily asks, "Where is he?"

Kabeer withholds the words that keep approaching his mouth and only whispers, "On the sofa, there." he gestures inside.

Ashraf gets inside the house, his pace slower now. Kabeer gets closer to his right ear and whispers, "He is different."

Ashraf spins around to face Kabeer. "Is he better?", he asks, disturbed. Kabeer sighs with pursed lips.

Without waiting any longer, Ashraf resumes pacing towards the sofa inside. The dusty, torn sofa is positioned adjacent to the wall at the far corner of the dimly lit room. There is no other furniture in the room except for a small round plastic table to the left of the sofa.

Taking slow and steady steps, he pushes himself towards the figure sitting on the sofa with his head drooping. The man is murmuring as he fidgets with his hands. Ashraf considers the white strands of hair that have now surpassed the few black strands on this man's head.

Time is funny.

"Anwar", his shivering voice echoes in the hall.

A moment passes. The man lifts his head and raises it to stare at Ashraf's gaping eyes.

The look gives Ashraf a sharp twinge right in his heart.

Emptiness. Just emptiness.

Things can change from overflowing to void and all it takes is some time. Some flying time!

Gracefully projecting the wrinkles on his forehead, his face resembles a crushed paper. Ashraf's eyes fall on the scar on his upper lip.

The scar!

It was the only thing that reminded Ashraf of Anwar. *His Anwar.* Time seems sluggish as they both stare at each other. One staring in disbelief and the other staring in confusion.

A weak grin takes shape on the latter's face. Then without any warning, he goes back to murmuring obscure words glancing down at his fidgeting hands. Ashraf swallows the lump that has formed in his throat as he catches himself wanting to be out of this place. He takes two steps back before turning around to leave but discontinues when he sees Aishumma on the threshold wiping her eyes with the edges of the shawl draped over her head. She bites her lower lip as tears roll down.

"He does not remember anything. I don't know how he got back here. He does not even look at me, Ashru", she says, her voice dampened by the tears.

***

"What did you say to your Ummi?" Anwar asks as he lowers himself to lay with his back against the powdery soft sea sand.

"I said I have an art competition at school within two days so I'll have to get the work done soon. So I am going to stay with Anwar today", grins Ashraf.

Anwar shakes his head, mockingly.

"What! You asked me to get outside *somehow*", Ashraf grumbles.

"No. it's just... it was genius", Anwar continues to keep the sarcasm in place.

"Oh! You had a better idea?" Ashraf rolls his eyes.

"Your Ummi knows you would not draw a line if I am around. She says that I am your greatest distraction from anything good"

Ashraf glances back at the dark but moonlit sea, smiling. It was his first time near the sea at night.

The wave sound seems sharper at night and the lapping sound of the waves creates a soothing sensation in him. The sea foam comes and retreats endlessly and his eyes feast on the magnificence. The moon is giving a weird sensation of happiness in him like a sedative drug. He suddenly finds himself wanting to be here every day like this. He knew nobody else could take any of his wishes the way this one person takes.

"I want to know what the sea looks like at night", Ashraf staunchly said to Anwar a few days ago.

They both managed to sneak out earlier this day before Ashraf's Uppa got back home.

An hour passes as they both immerse in their sea of thoughts. Half an hour past midnight, Ashraf begins to stir and shoves Anwar.

"You done?" Anwar asks, without taking his eyes off the vast starry sky.

"AH", Ashraf drawls.

They both take a leisurely walk on the vacant roads; mocking people, laughing, kicking each other. Just when they close in on the lane to his house, Anwar gets distracted. Ashraf turns to find Anwar a few steps behind him. He runs his eyes to the place where Anwar is staring. A flex banner showing a picture of pouting Silk Smitha is stretched on a stand at the top of a two-story building. Feeling his friend's eyes on him, Anwar says,

"This picture annoys me every day" Then he bends to pick a large stone from the road.

"What are you doing? Anwar, somebody would..." Before Ashraf could genuinely protest Anwar hurls the stone at the elevated banner.

Whatever happens next happens so fast that neither of them fully realizes the situation at the moment.

A thud sound is followed by a yelp. Then silence! Ashraf is still staring at the banner where Silk resumes to pout unharmed. Confused, he turns back to Anwar. He thinks Anwar is laughing. That must be why he is doubled over. But a frown overtakes his face when he notices traces of blood gliding on the hand that cups Anwar's mouth.

"Anwar?", Ashraf whispers, alarmed.

Anwar stands tall to face Ashraf and slowly moves his hand away from his mouth, revealing a deep cut on his upper lip with blood lavishly pouring out. Ashraf swallows seeing Anwar's blood-stained teeth and jaw. He hurriedly unbuttons his shirt.

Dropping his shirt on the road, he lifts his undershirt and wipes the dripping blood from the latter's jaw before pressing the undershirt onto Anwar's mouth. Anwar says something but the words are incomprehensible causing Ashraf to detach the cloth from his mouth.

"The stone...I think, it... rebounded off the banner and came back at me... I think", Anwar stammers.

Ashraf could have nodded. Or said something to pacify him. Or remained silent. But he guffaws.

"That picture annoys me every day. Right?" he taunts him. "Good thing! Since you have destroyed it completely, it won't *annoy* you anymore"

Ashraf could not stop laughing all night and got many laughing stitches. He laughs, not knowing his life is about to change. He laughs, not knowing he would never laugh like this in his entire life.

After that day, Anwar did not come looking for him for an entire week. It's not likely for him to stay away like this. School hours and family gatherings keep Ashraf on his toes in the coming days. On Sunday he says to his mother that he has to go see Anwar and asks her not to drag him into family huddles that day. She reluctantly agrees.

Anwar and Ashraf are sitting on the mango tree near Salaamikka's house, their legs dangling. Salaamikka is Anwar's uncle who has taken care of him after his parents died when he was just two years old.

It's pouring. Each wind that brushes against them chills their whole damp body. They silently regard people running to nearby sheds and shops. Ashraf peeks at his friend. Anwar is sitting with his face up towards the sky, eyes closed as though feeling every drop that falls on him. The cut has been healed but it has left a sharp trace on his upper lip. Ashraf suddenly remembers writing in his diary that Anwar is the only person in his life he holds in awe of, probably because of his friend's zeal and contented mind set. It was a privilege for him to be around Anwar, for he felt a certain level of importance when other boys in the village saw them together.

"Kids! Get inside!", Thommachan shouts from his tea shop.

"I think I better leave", says Ashraf. It's been almost an hour since they were on the tree and Anwar seems oddly quiet today. Ashraf wonders if it has something to do with his immoderate laughing when he cut his lips the last time they met.

"Salaam maama is dying", Anwar's words come as a blow.

"What!", Ashraf immediately asks, taken aback.

"you heard me"

"How? I mean...what happened? What is happening?"

"I overheard him talking to his doctor yesterday. And I heard him say it."

"I... umm...what about Aishumma? She knows?"

"I don't know."

A moment passes as Ashraf comprehends the entirety of the information. Aishumma is Salaamikka's wife who can barely walk due to disc problems in her spine. Ashraf wonders how she is taking the news.

"I will run away", Anwar comments, tersely.

"What!" Ashraf yells.

"You heard me"

"Of course, I heard you. I am not deaf! Now tell me, 'what for?'"

"He says he has a friend in UP who could get me a job."

"NO!" Ashraf shouts, finding his friend's words too overwhelming. "That's a long way from all of us. From *me*... What about school? You can stay with me. In my home... I ... will talk to my parents."

Anwar snickers before shaking his head as they both know the futility of the statement. Silence falls upon them again.

Pouring has now come down to drizzling. Ashraf is now grateful for the rain, for the water sliding and dripping from his face shrouds his tears. The road slowly becomes alive as people resume walking on the road again.

"I don't want you to leave. We will think of something like always." Ashraf descends from the branch. Wiping his face with his palms, he glances up at Anwar, who has now opened his eyes.

With his face still upturned towards the sky, Anwar says in a quivering voice,

"Don't come looking for me, Ashru. I mean it"

And Ashraf did.

Anwar disappeared long before the death of Salaam maama. No one cried or cared except for Ashraf and Aishumma. In his twenties, Ashraf travelled high and low of UP to find his best friend but only to fail.

Anwar disappeared.

***

A touch on his forehead jolts Ashraf's whole body and he opens his eyes rather painfully.

"You're sweating", his wife says in a low tone.

"I could've tried hard, Arifa. I *should've* tried hard", Ashraf murmurs suddenly. "I should've taken him to my home. He does not even recognize me, Arifa"

It takes a moment before Arifa can grasp his words. Settling her hand on his, she squeezes it mildly. It hurts her to see the reddening of his eyes.

"You did what you could. He did not want to be discovered. That's why he lied to you about some friend of his uncle and spent his entire life somewhere in a forest alone", Arifa defences her husband.

"Yes. But why? He did not want any trouble for Aishumma. Or me. He knew I would go to any extent to keep him with me", his words come as shouting.

At dinner, he shoves every morsel into him, for the regret weighs too heavy in his heart. Then he spends hours sitting on the front porch gazing at the darkness around. Arifa calls him inside a couple of times but he declines. When he finally returns to bed he finds his wife in deep sleep on the far side of the bed. He silently lowers himself near her and stretches himself on the bed. His sleepy eyes gently seal only to see the charming wide eyes of young Anwar forty-five years ago.

V
Alavi

BILAL CONTINUES TO pull the white scarf around his father's neck, causing the latter's stance to skew a bit. Scowling, Bilal stamps his foot on the bus stop persistently. Uneasiness unfolds in him when Alavi catches two ladies commenting on his son's conduct.

Latheefa stares at her son in vexation. Gesturing for her husband to disregard his tantrum, she turns to her right and anticipates the bus to Palakkad. The only bench in the unshielded bus stop is luxuriously occupied by an elderly couple and a girl child. The girl child is holding a Balarama book to her face just below her eyes. But her eyes wander away from the book and fall on Bilal repetitively. The blistering heat saps the energy and also the positive mood of the people.

Bilal has now started sobbing; managing to murmur in between his sobs. People seem to strive to maintain their patience as the resounding wails of Bilal continue to fill the sweltering jam-packed bus stop.

Latheefa suppresses once again the growing desire to give a nice whack at her son's back. Occupying a corner of the bus stop with her husband and son, she lets go of a long sigh as she keeps reminding herself that one slap in public would mean nights of explanation and compromising to her husband and her son too.

"Never embarrass a person in public. It would stay with him like a scar", Alavi once said to her.

But her patience is faltering now. She pulls the slipping pallu of her saree over to her forehead and tucks it behind her ears, hiding the sweaty, curly hair strands sticking onto her forehead.

Alavi is distracted from the draining heat and the displeasure his son is creating in others.

He regards the tears rolling down his son's face. Bilal wipes his runny nose with the back of his hand, spreading mucus lavishly beneath his nose. A lady scrunches her nose in disgust and looks away from the father and son.

Alavi rummages his shirt's pocket. The pale, stained off-white shirt hangs loosely on him as though it is hanging on a hanger. He mentally counts the coins without taking the money out of his pocket. He pauses. Pursing his lips, he glances at his wife.

Sweating profusely, Latheefa frowns beneath the wet saree pallu sticking onto her forehead. *The scorching sun and brewing frustration.* She sighs.

'*She knows*', Alavi contemplates.

"Come. Come", Alavi says, trying to get hold of his son's hand. "Let's get it"

The sound of Bilal's sobbing suddenly begins to ebb. It has now abated to occasional sniffs. Bilal wipes his face and runny nose, only adding to the disarray on his face. Alavi grabs his son's wrist before they cross the road. The hot wind that sweeps past them causes Alavi's loose shirt to flutter. Latheefa infuriatingly gazes at the duo, crossing the road and heading to the cramped and chaotic toy shop, opposite the bus stop.

"Spoiled brat made by spoiling father", a comment from an onlooker at the bus stop lingers in the air and gives rise to soft murmurings as consents to the comment.

Latheefa shuts her eyes and lets the embarrassment settle deep in her stomach pit. The patience and reasoning she has been holding onto all this time suddenly get lost and fail to find the way to her mind. She squeezes the saree pallu in her hand and impatiently waits for her husband and son to get back to her so that she can whack not her son's back but her son's stubborn head!

I'll show them that my son is not a spoiled brat and my husband is not a spoiling father!

It was Bilal who got out of the shop first. His eyes search for his mother's face. And when he spots his mother, his jaw drops in concern. A moment later, Alavi comes into the light and instantly notices Latheefa's piercing gaze at Bilal. He bows his head and smiles while letting out a soft snort. Moving closer to his son, he grabs Bilal's shoulder and side-hugs him. Then he brings his eyes to his wife and grins, waiting.

The frown still grips her face. But the grin shining from the other side relaxes her grip on her saree a bit. She slowly smiles. But the frown stays on.

At the boarding school, Latheefa and Alavi let their son pass through the huge gate, while they stayed behind. The heat remains fierce but cool winds now pass more frequently. The sweaty shirt sticks to Alavi's back. Hands-on hip, he regards his son walking to his classroom. Pausing at the entrance of his classroom, Bilal turns to the two distant figures behind the gate and waves at them. Beaming, he shoves the newly acquired grey football into his bag and swings the bag around his shoulders before disappearing into the classroom.

Alavi and Latheefa have refrained from talking to each other after Alavi has gone to the toy shop.

"You don't have enough money to get us back home, right?" Latheefa asks, plainly.

"Which means we'll have a long romantic walk before we get home", Alavi cheerfully responds, his smile revealing his smoke-tainted and degraded teeth.

He sees it but abstains from mentioning it because he fears that a tiny curve forming on either side of Latheefa's lips would vanish. He fears that the vanished frown will take their place again. Thus, he covertly adores her unwinding, without averting his gaze from her.

*****

Decades slip away stealing things on their way and everyone stands as a helpless onlooker.

In his seventies, Alavi laboured to wear his potent smile. His consistent coughing shook him off the zeal his wife once marvelled.

Every Friday Alavi's daughters come to visit him without fail. All three of them.

This Friday is no different. Gathering around Alavi, his daughters get immersed in the world of their father. Shahira wipes away the dust on the window sills. Haleema softly holds her father's pigmented, frail toes to cut the extended nails while Saahina arranges his tablets on a broken plastic container. Saahina places the container near an aged notebook on the wooden table. Suddenly she gets wandered away by the final words written within the diary's pages.

"In all my years, I have never seen your Uppa frustrated with any of you. If I can promise you anything, it would be this my children- no one can ever love you the way he does. Take care of him while you still can. Ummi."

Shaheena feels a pain tightening in her heart.

Bilal leans onto the door frame, his head lowered to face the new smartphone in his hand. He makes sure he keeps a fair distance from the foul-scented bed. He lets out an annoyed breath. It has been minutes and his father has not yet made it clear what he wants to eat.

"What should I get, Uppa?" he asks, feigning nonchalance.

Alavi gulps down the coarseness in his mouth. His sunken reddened eyes manage to open a little, and his threadbare brown body shines as though oiled richly.

"Idly", Alavi mumbles softly, his hollow-cheeked face striving to bring a smile but fails.

Bilal spins around and hurries to head out, his hand touching his shirt pocket to make sure he has taken the wallet.

"No. not idli. I want dosa.", Alavi makes a weathered rasping sound.

Bilal halts abruptly. He does not turn around to the room behind him. After a moment he takes a few more steps away from the room where his father is fading.

"No son. I want idli", Alavi craves the taste of anything more than just eating anything.

Bilal's ears get heated up. He purses his lips together tightly.

"Can you fix on something?" he achieves to make more sound than his father.

Bilal ignores the glares his sisters are shooting at him. He rolls his eyes thinking of the discipline lessons he would soon get. He impatiently waits with an exasperated gaze.

"Dosa", Alavi whispers. Bilal wrinkles his face because he could not hear his father's reply properly.

"Dosa!" Haleema makes it clear to him through clenched teeth, hatred towards her brother foaming inside her. Bilal storms out of the house.

This time Alavi smiles. He smiles, revealing his toothless gums. He smiles with wet eyes. *He smiles.*

VI
Mopping Cloth

A COBWEB STRETCHES from the window sill to the wooden frame of the window. When the wind blows against it, the web wavers like a grotesque skeleton hand dancing.

Like the movie I just saw at Jaffer's house

Staring at the swaying cobweb in his home with a despondent heart, Khaleel muses what just happened.

Those sharp rose thorns!

Khaleel suddenly remembers how he got pricked by one when he sneaked through the garden and surreptitiously watched the Hotel Transylvania movie that played on the huge TV viewable from the house's large glass panes. The vivid moves on the big screen made Khaleel overlook why he sneaked into the giant house's garden. Dazzling pictures passed Khaleel's mind for a while even after he took his eyes off the giant box that took an ample portion of the wall in the hall. He, nevertheless, could regain his mind over his mission swiftly. *His mission...*

Khaleel entering through the kitchen is not a peculiar thing. But the fact that he is visiting when he knows Jaffer is not there has the odd element. Jaffer's parents considered it as his humility. Several times they reprimanded him for the same.

"You are like our family, Khaleel. Next time come through the main entrance", Jaffer's Uppa once commanded. But his main entrance remained the kitchen door.

Jaffer had come to his little home a few days back to inform him about their absence for a week. He informed Khaleel that he and his Ummi were accompanying his Uppa for his business meeting in Bangalore. And just that moment Khaleel thought,

Now or never.

Khaleel mounts the steps that lead to the store room at the back of the kitchen. His heart anxiously beats as he sneaks into the kitchen. He peeks at the giant dining room for any signs of living bodies. When he finds none, he desperately jiggles the storeroom handle and opens it.

His eyes search wildly around the room. Then those wide eyes land on the mopping sticks hanging cosily from nooks on the far corner of the wall; five mopping sticks with attached cloths on them. All sorts! Two string mops, three flat mops and all with elegant cloths attached. There are also small square microfiber clothes hanging on a cloth line inside the room.

How can a mopping rod look so classy?

His widened eyes then start to desperately run in every corner as though searching for something more. Not a trace of a T-shirt or pants turned to a cleaning rag, or any slimy tattered clothes in any corner of the room.

Disappointment sinks his heart and pulls his head down. He shuffles out of the back door without noticing Seydhukka gaping at him at the threshold of the kitchen. Seythukka has just entered the house after gardening. He stands confused thinking why the little figure had been inspecting the storeroom.

Khaleel paces tediously back home.

At home, he suddenly recollects what his teacher said about the significance of deep breathing when uptight. Glancing up at his mother mopping the floor, he lets go of a deep sigh.

Fathima wrings the dingy blue t-shirt; water leaking to the brown bucket underneath. Placing the rag on the flat mop head, she continues to bathe the floor.

Khaleel regards the torn cloth and suddenly finds himself in need of another sigh. But frustration restrains him from having one. The loss of the bright blue colour anguishes him not as much as the t-shirt's transition to a mopping rag.

"Ummi", Khaleel whispers, his eyes unwavering from the dreary rag.

"Hm?" Fathima pants while she forcefully moves the cloth across the floor.

"I never see Jaffer's shirts used for cleaning in his house", Khaleel says softly.

Fathima frowns not looking away from her work. When Khaleel finds his mother not turning to him, he cries, "Ummi!"

"Huh? So? What about it?" Fathima speaks while panting.

"Why can't we buy one?"

"Buy what?"

"A mopping rod."

"We have one", Fathima spins around to let her son see the rod in her hand, slanting it dramatically. And then returns to mopping in a hurry.

"But that needs my shirts. My pants. Get one with an attached cloth. Can we?" Khaleel pleads as he gulps down the ache in his throat.

"Next day I will use my nighties and shawls. Will that solve the problem? I will bury your old shirts and all then. There's no space here on the shelf to keep your torn clothes too", she says, nonchalantly.

"Why do we have to use our clothes, Ummi", Khaleel says, suddenly feeling embarrassed as the stifled emotions in him caused his voice to crack. He suppresses the tears with amplified effort.

I am thirteen. How will she react if I cry?

"These are our old clothes. What's the big deal?" she asks.

"But... once we used them. Can we buy a new good mopping rod? Please", he pleads.

"We have a good one!" Fathima raises her voice to stress the matter, "These are our old clothes. Why do you feel suddenly concerned about these torn clothes? 'Good for nothing' clothes!"

"Good for nothing, right? Then burn it. Or bury it, like you said. But don't do this..." Wrinkling his face, Khaleel circles his index finger around the dirt-amassed cloth rag on the floor.

Mila, their cat casually walks into the house, staining the wet floor with muddy paw marks. Fathima gives off a howl and in a flash swings the rod in its direction, close enough to startle it and distant enough not to harm it. Mila bolts outside and disappears.

"See, how this rod helped me now! What would I have done without it", Fathima laughs, melodramatically pulling the rod close to her.

Khaleel turns to his other side to face the backrest of the sofa as a protest to his Mother's wisecrack.

Fathima giggles as she revisits in her mind the conversation they had just now.

"Why, my son? Why bother about these silly things? We don't have the money to buy new things as and when we want. We can only buy new things when we are in desperate need of it. I can't even afford to give you an education" Fathima's smile steadily fades and a deep frown becomes her key facial feature.

"I don't know how I would have sent you to school if it hadn't been for Hamad ikka. You should always be grateful to Jaffer for it. He is the one who persuaded his Uppa to give you a sponsorship education." Ummi wets the cloth again and begins wiping the space under their dining table.

Feeling disquiet, Khaleel closes his eyes shut. He is always grateful to Jaffer for everything.

Everything.

Jaffer was the first one to notice Khaleel was taking too much leave from school. He came home to ask about why Khaleel didn't get outside, fearing his friend had been ill. When Fathima lamented about her son's suspension due to unpaid fees at school, Jaffer did not stay there for long. He ran to his father and emphatically demanded to pay all the arrears in that year and all the years to come. His father did. Moreover, he was even admitted to Jaffer's school. And now, they both always sit together at school.

But that's not the issue! I don't see any of my friends having to witness the scene of their clothes turning to a cleaning rag.

Khaleel has asked almost all of his friends the same in one way or another.

He has already asked many.

"What do you do to your old clothes?",

"What happens when your clothes get torn or become old?",

"You see your clothes used for cleaning at home?"

And he always got answers like,

"Some we trash it and some we give for charity",

"I don't know! My mother put it away with the rubbish most times",

"Why? Your clothes are used for cleaning at your home? Mine...I don't know... I see my mom burning it sometimes."

Maybe it's because they are all well-off than me.

Khaleel sits up on the sofa with crossed legs. He regards the cleaned floor.

The corners of the floor are still damp; even the highest speed settings rotated the fan in a leisurely manner. Fathima's bare footprints on the mopped floor are observable from where Khaleel sits. Khaleel blames it on the mopping stick employing his t-shirt.

Water splashes off around the floor surrounding the bucket every time she wrings the cloth. Her hands turn whitish when she squeezes the damp cloth and becomes bright pink when she relaxes them. Khaleel blames it on the bleached t-shirt.

Fathims disappears to clean the kitchen floor. Remembering the grotesque hand, he glances in the direction of the window to the right of the sofa. Minutes pass as he re-enters the movie scenes in his head but it finally ends with the scene where he discovers the exclusive mopping sticks at Jaffer's.

Strangely he feels tired and his eyelids get heavy. Feeling grateful for the incoming sleepiness, he reclines back on the sofa and dozes off.

'Khaleel...' someone is calling me. But there is darkness everywhere.

I know that voice but how do I find the person? I can't see anything.

'Khaleel...'

"I am here. Here. I am here."

"I know you are there! Get up!" Khaleel recognizes his Mother's voice. "Why did you sleep now? So that you can skip lunch too?"

Laboriously opening his eyes, Khaleel pushes his hands against the sofa and sits up. His head jerks unconsciously towards the window. But his eyes immediately dart to the figure standing outside his front door.

I thought I woke up. Why am I still dreaming?

"Assalamu alaikkum. What's up, Khaleel man!" Jaffer hollers.

What is he doing in my dream? I am dreaming, right?

Seeing the perplexed face of his friend, Jaffer raises his right hand with his palms facing up to express his confusion.

Allah! I am not dreaming. He is really here!

Khaleel springs up and walks to the front door.

"You did not go to Bangalore? What are you doing here?", he sputters, pulling his loose waist of the shorts up. What he really meant was *'Did you see me sneaking around your house today?'*

"I said salam, Khaleel", Jaffers says slowly, rolling his eyes.

"aahhh... Walaikkumussalam", Khaleel cries before adding, "Why didn't you go?"

"So, you are upset because I did not leave you alone for some time?"

"No, Jaffer. I mean... You said you won't be here. Of course, I missed you. It's just... I mean... were you at home today morning?"

Jaffer nods, smiling.

"Seythukka said that you came home today. But he was surprised when you did not ask for me to anyone. Do you know why I was surprised? Why did you come home when you knew I wouldn't be home? Why did you stop at the kitchen?" Jaffer asks bringing his hands to his hip.

Khaleel would have noted his friend's new pants if the situation had not been this jarring. Jaffer knows he is a bad liar but he really needs to work something out now.

"I forgot about your trip. It is our normal routine when we don't have school. I remembered only when I got inside", Khaleel rushes his words to quickly finish the lie. He wanted to sigh but that would be odd now. So, he smiles at him instead.

"You seem weird today. You don't seem happy seeing me. Like... really happy!", Jaffer frowns.

The smile vanishes on Khaleel's face in a split second.

"Of course, I am happy seeing you. What are you saying! It's just the nap". Khaleel says with bulging eyes.

"Oh... the sleep inertia. Huh?" Jaffer drawls and gives out a chuckle. Khaleel nods, though it is not true, for he is feeling nervously alert more than the waking haziness.

A moment passes before Jaffer asks, "Now, will you move? I need to enter. Where's Ummi?"

Khaleel suddenly moves aside and waves his hand, gesturing for his friend to get inside.

"Ummi", Jaffer calls out. "Ummi", Khaleel joins in too. They both look at each other and chuckle.

"Jaffer!" ummi cries from the kitchen, "Come here, son"

Jaffer keeps a closet bag he has been holding in his hand on the sofa and goes round the table in the living room to get to the kitchen. It is only then Khaleel notices that Jaffer has been holding the cloth bag all this time. He was in absolute shock seeing Jaffer at this hour and he could not notice anything else.

Khaleel goes to the kitchen without giving much attention to the bag, for he wants to hear what the duo are discussing.

Fathima is sautéing onions for the beef curry. Plastic containers containing the spice powders are arranged in a circle near the stove. Crushed ginger and garlic, green chillies, a chopped tomato and curry leaves are laid out on the mildew-covered cutting board. A delicious aroma fills the kitchen as she deposits the set ingredients into the sautéed onions. Khaleel watches the curry preparation with a grumbling tummy while listening to their conversation. Jaffer discloses to Fathima that his Uppa, Hamad, asked him not to miss school this time as exams are nearing. That is why he could not go to Bangalore.

"Uppa says that eighth grade is a crucial turning point. He said we would go in the vacation time. Also, I had to do something", Jaffer says, glancing sideways at Khaleel. But the latter does not notice it, for his eyes are set on the pan.

Adding all the spices into the pan, Fathima begins sautéing the mix well to make it soft and squishy. Adding a glass of water to it, she then reduces the heat and allows it to simmer. Khaleel swallows the rising saliva in my mouth, for it is an empty stomach receiving the aromatic air of the kitchen.

"What is it? What did you have to do?" Fathima asks, running water on her hands to rid them of the spice powders and other stains from cooking.

"Have you finished cooking this mouth-watering curry?", Jaffer asks in return. Khaleel shoots a glance at him, for he was about to ask the same. Although Jaffer asked that for a whole different purpose.

"Haa. Why?" Ummi smiles at the compliment that came with the question.

Jaffer grabs her damp hand and leads her outside the kitchen. Khaleel, taken aback, pursues them, but only after wiping the curry-stained spoon laid on the steel stove top with his fingers and licking them keenly.

Jaffer unzips the cloth bag on the sofa he brought over while Fathima keeps asking about its contents. Taking out a neatly folded stack of clothes, he zips the bag closed and places it back on the sofa.

"These are your shirts and t-shirts, right?", Khaleel asks, amazed.

"Yes, these are mine.", answers Jaffer.

Thinking Jaffer has brought it all for him, he wipes his licked fingers over the t-shirt he has on to receive the gift.

Jaffer takes out the top three items of the bundle and outstretches them to Khaleel.

"These three are for you. These are my new shirts and one t-shirt", he says with a grin.

Khaleel eagerly acquires them and then he jerks his head towards the bottom pile.

"These are for Ummi", Jaffer says, excited.

Fathima is not the only one agape now. Khaleel too, for he is wondering why his Ummi is getting Jaffer's shirts.

"Son, I don't wear...these...", Fathima mumbles.

"What?" Jaffer frowns in surprise and then as if realizing the matter he straightaway clarifies, "This is not for you to wear."

"Then?" Fathima and Khaleel ask together in confusion.

"I bought these for mopping. You can get rid of the old ones and use these for mopping from now on", Jaffer is grinning when he says this.

But the other two people in the room don't.

"For mopping? You mean like...the floor, the table...?" Fathima inquires, still confused.

"Yes... anywhere you want. Just use them for something", Jaffer takes the bundle from the sofa and shakes it as a gesture to take it from him. Fathima complies and collects the clothes.

Khaleel starts to doubt again whether he really has woken up from his sleep. He impulsively glances down at the sofa to check if his body is still lying unconsciously on the sofa.

Nothing. Just his cloth bag.

Khaleel shakes his head for being silly.

"Why, Jaffer? What is wrong with these clothes? It looks great", he says in disbelief.

"See..." Jaffer grabs the topmost shirt and unfolds it, "There's a small tear in the pocket and the colour has faded"

He continues to unfold the shirts to reveal a trivial stain. Or an invisible tear. Or unseen lint.

Khaleel swallows, thinking 'What is this guy thinking!'

"But these are good clothes, son", Fathima says.

"Good ones I gave Khaleel. I haven't worn any of those. My ummi packs my used, good clothes for orphanages. But these are the rest. Ummi has kept these for burning in our backyard. But...", Jaffer glances at the bundle Fathima is holding.

"I never see my clothes used for cleaning. I envy Khaleel for that. He always gets to witness his clothes becoming a hero here in this home. My used clothes are burned. But I always watch how the clothes in this house serve different purposes. I see you, Ummi, using Khaleel's tattered shirt or t-shirt or trousers or pants for cleaning the kitchen counter, wiping the table top, dusting the windows and mopping the floor. I was surprised when I saw a piece of his blue floral shirt wrapped around your fingers a few days back. When I asked about it, you said that you had accidentally cut your fingers and had to cover it up to stop the bleeding. See..." he pauses and points at Fathima's right hand, where a long cut on her index finger and thumb has still not scabbed over.

Khaleel squints at the wound on his Mother's hand. He had seen the cut and suddenly remembers panicking when he saw the flowing blood. But he did not notice the piece his mother used to cover it afterwards. If he had, he would have definitely sulked for using his shirt piece for that too.

Turning to Khaleel, Jaffer gives a keen look at him before saying,

"Nothing you wear has vanished just like that", Jaffer snaps his fingers, "Every piece of cloth does some service before it disappears completely. You know, the purpose even a simple piece of your cloth assumes in this house amazes me. I like it."

Stunned by Jaffer's words, Khaleel stares at his friend in disbelief. He feels like he is desperately in need of another sigh now. He takes a deep breath; and slowly and steadily exhales it through his mouth.

Fortunately, this sigh unloads something heavy from his heart. He smiles at Jaffer.

Lowering the clothes in her hand back on the sofa, Fathima pulls Jaffer for a tight embrace. She then kisses him on the forehead with moist eyes. Khaleel's smile widens, watching them.

When Fathima loosens the hug, Jaffer glances up at her and says, "I would love to have that lunch towel you stitched with his t-shirt last year, that grey towel. But I am afraid my ummi would not approve."

Fathima laughs heartily with her hands on her shaking tummy as tears slide down her cheeks.

"Boys, get the plates and set the table. Let's have lunch together", Fathima orders, wiping her face with her palms.

Khaleel's eyes fall on the rusty bucket near the kitchen, filled with filthy water from mopping.

The stick with his soaked shirt at the mop head is kept slanting onto the wall adjacent to the bucket. He slants his head as he assumes the rod evolving into a fierce weapon; a weapon utilizing his shirt. He smiles at the thought, surprised at his change of mood. He is surprised that everything feels better in his home now.

Everything better. Just like that.

That night Khaleel folds his new clothes and arranges them on his shelf. He then extracts a pile of his old clothes. He has not set those aside even though they are worn out, for he feared his Mother would use them for cleaning. For some reason, he feels relieved that his Ummi had not mentioned the conversation they had earlier to Jaffer.

He is about to close the door of his wooden shelf when he notices the undisturbed cobwebs in the inside corners of the shelf; intact and still. Khaleel takes an old shirt at the top of the pile he has just withdrawn from the shelf and wipes the dusty web off his shelf.

"Gotcha!", Khaleel squeaks with glee as he runs to his Ummi.

VII
Beautiful Living

HOW COMPLEX IS life but how simple is living? Or is it like how simple is life but how complex is living? I think the answer varies. 'But how am I taking it?' is a question I explore every day after meeting him. And I will tell you how 'he' inspired me.

It is a Monday morning. I happened to be at the bus stop earlier today. Since it is only 6:30 in the morning, no living body can be seen around. The blue sky has only started brightening up to set the stage for the day. As I stand leaning on one of the pillars of the bus stop, oblivious to everything around me since my mind kept on playing and replaying the mischief my friends did to me the other day at college, a boy seeming the age of eleven approaches me.

"Will you buy a packet of candles?" the boy asks.

Only then did I become aware of his presence, eliciting a startled reflex from me. He has all the features of the rag pickers in my area; tattered clothes, messy hair, barefoot, dirty hands. I stare at him, speechless.

'I'll have to sell these packets by noon", he pleads, mistaking my startled silence for denial of his offer.

"Um... Hi...", I mumble, still sinking the impact of the surprise. "Why do you want to sell those by noon itself?"

"Because I don't think I would be even able to stand if I don't have anything to eat by noon. I haven't eaten anything since yesterday morning", he answers, his sound narrating the weariness in his body.

I don't instantly react. With an open mouth, I continue to glance at him, analyzing his words. Then my eyes widen and I give out a loud, "Oh" before I abruptly take out my lunch. Unsure of his response, I extend it towards him with a mind set to persuade him if he declines. The moment he understood that it is food I am offering, he drops the three candle packets in his hand and takes the box from me. Seating himself on the muddy cemented floor of the bus stop, he begins having his feast.

Ummi cooked rice and dal curry in the morning for my lunch today. *My favourite.*

I can't help but grin at the joy this little figure in front of me is exhibiting now. Questions rush to my mind and then I pick one to shoot at him.

"Where do you live?" I ask.

"Everywhere I am", comes his reply, astonishing me.

I find myself enjoying the spirit the kid carries with him. The rag he is wearing or the dirty hands do not dull the sparkle in his eyes a bit.

"Who gave you the candles?" I curiously shoot him the next one as he gobbles up his food.

"The old lady who sits at the front of that church every day", he says, pointing his food-covered hand behind me.

"You...are...happy, right?" I stammer. I just wanted to hear his reply.

"I always am", he says in between the bouts of hiccups. "Do you have water, Dhi?"

I smile at him.

Maybe it's the way he called me 'dhi'.

As I pull the water bottle from my bag, I ask, "You're happy even when hungry all day?"

I wait impatiently for his answer as he drinks ravenously.

"Aaah. Why not? That hunger pushes me forward. It keeps me going in a way. Every day is like a new experience. Different kinds of chaps I meet every day...different...Some are rude to me when I approach them and some are ignorant. But that's OK. You know Dhi, my Ammi once told me that I don't ever have to be sad thinking I don't have a normal life like many of you people. Unlike most of the people we see every day who are living mainly for money, power and status, we have freedom. We are relieved of all the unnecessary pressure of normal living. That's what she said. I am free, you know. Nobody sees me, like really sees me. Nobody knows me or cares about me. I am not answerable to anyone, right?" he says every line with such an assertion that I can't help but wonder,

'How is he even possible?'

I don't respond to his words. Rather, I stand staring at him contemplating the deep words.

"I am sorry, Dhi, that you don't have that freedom like me.", he says bringing his eyes to mine. My mouth wide opens. His eyes say it; that he meant what he just said. I chuckle before saying, "Seriously!"

He glances back down at my lunch box and starts finger-picking the box.

"My Ammi was always happy. I am not as great as her in that though. I remember the smile on her face when she died" he says, as if to himself.

I find myself wanting to sit beside him and pat on his shoulders but the filthy floor beneath my feet halts me. Pushing himself off the floor, he washes his hands and my lunch box using my water bottle. I keep peeking at him when I put my things back in my bag.

Bending his head forward, he wipes his face on the bottom of his dusty shirt. When he notices me eyeing him, he smiles at me with his thin lips. I reply with a closed-lip smile.

"I love watching people. I see different people every day. From the old lady at the church to the man in suit and tie who once spat at me when I asked to buy the candles." He bends down to pick up the candles he dropped earlier. Bringing his glance back up to me, he continues with a widened smile, "I wish I would live a thousand years more so that I would see and experience more and more people every day. And one day I would call out to the world how people have become indifferent and uncaring. Don't you think?"

I swallow, taken aback by the enormity of his words. I start to feel slightly embarrassed to stand in front of this little guy with an impressive perception about life, for I haven't ever thought like that, let alone talk like that.

"Wow", I manage to say.

I start rummaging through my bag and dig out some coins and notes.

"Here, take it", I say.

When he brings his palm up, I press the money onto it. I buy all the candles from him. And when he says that the money is too much I ask him to keep it. The glee on his face is worth the money. Though I have questions brimming in me, I keep gazing at his childish face silently. I keep gazing at the zeal on that face even after having nobody to call on his own.

He takes a few steps away from me before turning back to look at me. And I suppose that he is about to say 'thank you' or a 'bye'.

"You are like the old lady at the church who gives me free candles to sell. When I become a big businessman, I will return the favour. Mind you, I would never do things like the one who spat on my face". Yes, that was a 'thank you' note from him.

I laugh out loud. I watch him walk away humming an unfamiliar tune.

The loud beep of the bus honk brings my mind back to my *routine* life. I start to ponder on the kid's words and all the questions I never asked him. But that's OK, for I feel like he left something in me; something bright I might need to hold on in my life. Oh, wait...

What was his name?